Words that appear in **bold** type are defined in the glossary on pages 28 and 29.

Please visit our web site at: www.garethstevens.com
For a free color catalog describing Gareth Stevens Publishing's
list of high-quality books and multimedia programs, call
1-800-542-2595 (USA) or 1-800-387-3178 (Canada).
Gareth Stevens Publishing's fax: (414) 332-3567.

Library of Congress Cataloging-in-Publication Data

Baumbusch, Brigitte.
    Cats in art / by Brigitte Baumbusch.
       p. cm. — (What makes a masterpiece?)
    Includes index.
    ISBN 0-8368-4444-0 (lib. bdg.)
       1. Cats in art—Juvenile literature. I. Title.
    N7668.C3B38   2005
    704.9'4329752—dc22   2004057441

This edition first published in 2005 by
Gareth Stevens Publishing
A WRC Media Company
330 West Olive Street, Suite 100
Milwaukee, Wisconsin 53212 USA

Copyright © Andrea Dué s.r.l. 2003

This U.S. edition copyright © 2005 by Gareth Stevens, Inc.
Additional end matter copyright © 2005 by Gareth Stevens, Inc.

Translator: Erika Pauli

Gareth Stevens series editor: Dorothy L. Gibbs
Gareth Stevens art direction: Tammy West

Printed in the United States of America

1 2 3 4 5 6 7 8 9 09 08 07 06 05

CATS in Art

by Brigitte Baumbusch

GARETH**STEVENS**
GS
PUBLISHING
A WRC Media Company

What makes a cat...

This majestic **bronze sculpture** is about 2,600 years old. It was made in **ancient** Egypt, where cats were held in high **esteem**. This cat has gold earrings and is wearing a fancy collar and **amulet** around its neck, just as many people did at that time in history.

Everyone knows that kittens will play with anything that moves. This furry kitten chasing a butterfly is a modern Chinese **embroidery**.

a masterpiece?

Some cats fight...

Francisco Goya, one of Spain's greatest artists, painted these two **scrappy** cats on a wall (above) more than two centuries ago.

and some are friends.

This loving pair of kittens is a drawing by Andy Warhol, who was a **contemporary** American artist.

Cats can be poor . . .

A quiet kitten keeps these two **vagabonds** company as they share their **meager** meal. The painting is by Giacomo Ceruti, an eighteenth-century Italian artist who often **portrayed** the lives of the poor.

French artist Pierre Bonnard painted this **haughty** white cat more than a century ago.

or proud.

There are black cats . . .

Théophile-Alexandre Steinlen, a Swiss-born artist, had a **fascination** for cats. In the late 1800s, he made this black cat with a lacy **halo** (left) for a Paris **cabaret** named "Le Chat Noir," which means "The Black Cat."

white cats . . .

This sleepy white cat is a Japanese hand warmer made of **porcelain**.

In 1913, Franz Marc painted these three cats (above) in different colors and poses. Marc, a German artist, was extraordinarily fond of animals.

cats in all colors . . .

and even striped cats.

This unusual cat with colored stripes was painted in a **medieval** Irish book more than 1,200 years ago.

About one hundred years ago, French painter Henri
Rousseau portrayed this striped **tabby** in a pose looking
much like its owner's.

Cats can be
embroidered . . .

An imaginative blue cat was carefully embroidered on this nineteenth-century wool rug from North America.

This charming cat face was drawn in about 1930 by French writer Jean Cocteau as an invitation to a "friends of cats" club.

or written.

Some cats talk . . .

Felix (above) is one of quite a few cats who are the stars of famous comics and cartoons. Created in the 1920s, he is portrayed here by American **pop artist** Andy Warhol.

This chorus of cats is a humorous painting by a seventeenth-century Flemish artist named David Teniers, who enjoyed painting animals engaged in human activities.

others sing.

Cats can be thoughtful . . .

In this **watercolor**, a staring cat appears to have a bird on its mind. It was painted in 1928 by Swiss artist Paul Klee.

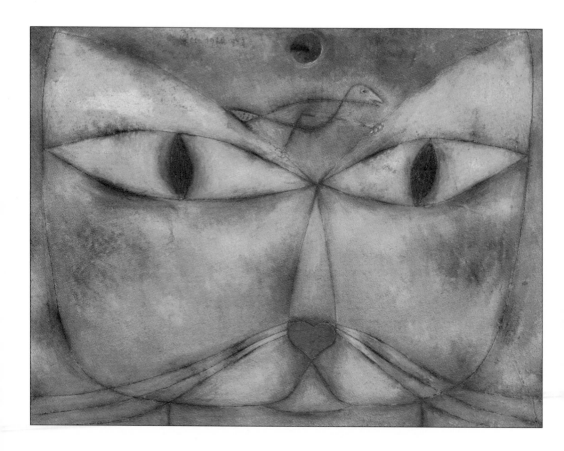

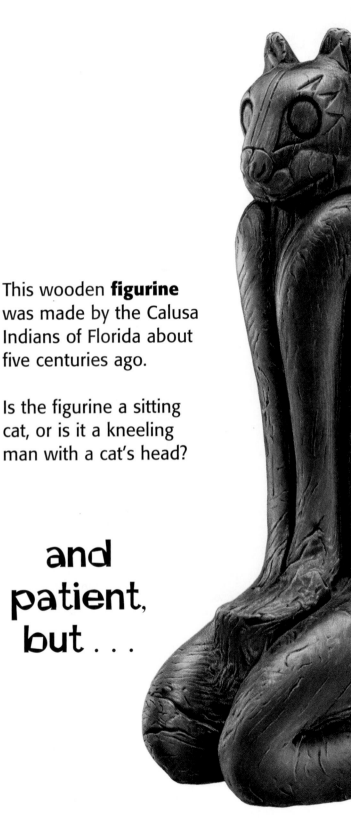

This wooden **figurine** was made by the Calusa Indians of Florida about five centuries ago.

Is the figurine a sitting cat, or is it a kneeling man with a cat's head?

and patient, but . . .

some cats are wild!

This **pendant** of gold is very old. It was made in about the first century by Native peoples in what is now the country of Colombia. It might be a jaguar or some other kind of wildcat, but it is not a house cat.

Who doesn't recognize this smiling face? It is the Cheshire Cat from Lewis Carroll's *Alice's Adventures in Wonderland* as it appears in Walt Disney's animated feature film *Alice in Wonderland*.

Some cats will just sit and smile.

Some cats travel.

In this picture, painted in the nineteenth century by American artist George Caleb Bingham, a cat is accompanying two **fur traders** who are traveling down the Missouri river with their **pelts**.

All cats hunt...

Cats have made themselves useful hunting mice ever since they first began to live with people — as long ago as ancient Egypt, where this wooden toy was made more than 3,000 years ago.

In this illustration from an English **bestiary** of more than seven centuries ago, three cats present a mouse almost as if it were a gift.

mice . . .

This cat with a rat
in its mouth (above)
is from a picture
painted five centuries
ago by Dutch artist
Hieronymus Bosch.

but not when
they are sleeping.

The nineteenth-century Japanese drawing below somewhat illustrates the old saying that when the cat's away — or, in this case, asleep — the mice play.

GLOSSARY

amulet
a charmlike ornament with a figure, symbol, or words on it, which was believed to have magical powers that could protect the wearer from harm, illness, or evils, such as witchcraft

ancient
relating to a period in history from the earliest civilizations until about the time of the Roman Empire

bestiary
a type of book in medieval times that contained descriptions of animals or a fable (a story that presents a truth, moral, or lesson) about real or imaginary animals

bronze
a hard metal alloy (combination of two or more metals) that is a mixture of mainly copper and tin

cabaret
a nightclub or restaurant that provides late-night entertainment, especially performances that include singing and dancing

contemporary
relating to a person or an event living or happening in current or modern times

embroidery
decorative needlework that uses artistic stitches to form figures and designs

esteem
an opinion of honor, value, or worth, usually with regard to a person

fascination
a strong attraction toward something that is very hard, if not impossible, to resist

figurine
a small, decorative, statuelike figure, usually made of china, pottery, wood, or metal

fur traders
hunters who trap or kill animals for their fur so they can trade or sell the pelts

halo
a circle of light that surrounds the head of an angel or some other glorified being

haughty
proud to the extent of looking down on others and often being offensively loud and showy

meager
lacking in quantity, and often in quality; simple in content and small in amount

medieval
belonging to the Middle Ages, a period of history in Europe from the end of the Roman Empire to the 1500s

pelts
animal skins that have been removed from the animals with the fur or hair still attached

pendant
a type of necklace that is usually a charm or small ornament hanging from a chain

pop artist
an artist whose work features everyday objects, such as soup cans and road signs, either as subjects or media (the physical materials used to create a work of art)

porcelain
a delicate white ceramic material used to make fine china dishes and figurines

portrayed
pictured, especially in the style of a portrait, with just the head, neck, and shoulders or partial upper body showing

scrappy
high spirited and aggressive, as if trying to start a fight

sculpture
a work of art created by carving, modeling, or molding materials such as wood, rock, stone, clay, or metal into a figure or object that is three-dimensional, instead of flat

tabby
a type of house cat with a striped coat that is a combination of light and dark colors

vagabonds
wanderers; unsettled, homeless people who move from place to place, often begging or stealing food and clothing to meet even their most basic needs

watercolor
a painting technique that uses paints or pigments (colorings) that dissolve in water, rather than in oil, often resulting in softer, less defined figures and backgrounds

page 4 – Bronze statue of a seated cat. Egyptian art of the Late Period, after 600 B.C., from Saqqara. London, British Museum. Drawing by Sauro Giampaia.

page 5 – Kitten chasing a butterfly, detail of an embroidery. Chinese art of the 20th century. Private property. Drawing by Sauro Giampaia.

pages 6-7 – Francisco Goya (1746-1828): Cats Brawling on a Wall. Madrid, Prado. Museum photo.

page 7 – Andy Warhol (1930-1987): Two seated kittens, ink drawing, 1954. New York, The Andy Warhol Foundation for the Visual Arts. Photo Art Resource / Scala. © Andy Warhol by SIAE, 2003.

page 8 – Giacomo Ceruti (1700-1768): The Two Vagabonds. Brescia, Pinacoteca Civica. Photo Scala Archives.

page 9 – Pierre Bonnard (1867-1947): The White Cat, 1894. Paris, Musée d'Orsay. Photo RMN. © Pierre Bonnard by SIAE, 2003.

page 10 – Théophile-Alexandre Steinlen (1859-1923): Black cat, drawing for a poster for the cabaret "Le Chat Noir." Paris, Bibliothèque des Arts décoratifs. Drawing by Sauro Giampaia.

Glazed porcelain hand warmer in the form of a sleeping cat. Japanese art of the 20th century. Kyoto, National Museum. Drawing by Sauro Giampaia.

page 11 – Franz Marc (1880-1916): Three Cats, 1913. Münster, Westfälisches Landesmuseum. Photo Joachim Blauel / Artothek.

page 12 – Miniature of a cat, from the "Book of Kells." Medieval Irish art of the late 8th century. Dublin, Trinity College Library. Drawing by Sauro Giampaia.

page 13 – Henri Rousseau (1844-1910): Portrait of Pierre Loti, c. 1910. Zurich, Kunsthaus. Photo Claus Hansmann / Artothek.

page 14 – Blue cat, detail of an embroidered rug. American folk art of the 19th century. New York, Metropolitan Museum of Art. Drawing by Sauro Giampaia.

page 15 – Jean Cocteau (1889-1963): Drawing of a cat for the "Club des amis des chats," 1930. © Jean Cocteau by SIAE, 2003.

page 16 – Andy Warhol (1930-1987): Felix the Cat, lithograph, 1985-86. New York, The Andy Warhol Foundation for the Visual Arts. Photo Art Resource / Scala. © Andy Warhol by SIAE, 2003.

page 17 – David Teniers the Younger (1610-1690): Concert of Cats and Monkeys, detail. Munich, Bayerische Staatsgemäldesammlungen. Photo Joachim Blauel / Artothek.

page 18 – Paul Klee (1879-1940): Cat and Bird, 1928. New York, Museum of Modern Art. Photo Museum of Modern Art / Scala. © Paul Klee by SIAE, 2003.

page 19 – Wooden figurine with feline head. Calusa Indians of Florida, late Mississippi or early historical period, 1400-1600, from Key Macro. Washington, National Museum of Natural History, Smithsonian Institution. Drawing by Sauro Giampaia.

page 20 – Gold pendant in the shape of a feline. Sinu culture, 150 B.C. to A.D. 900, from Uraba (Colombia). Bogotá, Museo de Oro. Photo RMN / Rudolf Schirimpff.

page 21 – The Cheshire Cat, from the animated feature film *Alice in Wonderland*, has been reproduced with the kind permission of The Walt Disney Company. Photo Disney Publishing Worldwide. © Disney Enterprises, Inc.

pages 22-23 – George Caleb Bingham (1811-1879): Fur Traders Descending the Missouri. New York, Metropolitan Museum of Art. Photo Bridgeman / Farabolafoto.

pages 24-25 – Wooden toy of a cat chasing mice. Egyptian art of the New Kingdom, 1550-1070 B.C., from Thebes. London, British Museum. Drawing by Sauro Giampaia.

page 25 – Illustration of three cats and a rat, miniature from the *Harleian Bestiary*. Medieval English art of the 13th century. London, British Library. Drawing by Sauro Giampaia.

page 26 – Hieronymus Bosch (1450-1516): Detail from the left wing of the Triptych of the Garden of Earthly Delights. Madrid, Prado. Photo Scala Archives.

pages 26-27 – Kawanabe Kyosai (1831-1889): Cat and mouse, ink and watercolor. New York, Metropolitan Museum of Art. Drawing by Sauro Giampaia.

INDEX